Let's Go, Panthers!

Aimee Aryal

Illustrated by Miguel De Angel

with Brad Vinson

www.mascotbooks.com

It was a beautiful fall day in the Carolinas. Panthers fans from all over the area were making their way to the stadium to watch their Panthers play football.

All over town, everyone dressed in Panthers colors. As fans made their way to the stadium, they cheered, "Let's go, Panthers!"

Hours before the start of the game, Panthers fans began gathering at the stadium. The smell of good food was in the air as smoke billowed from grills. Sir Purr, the Panthers mascot, joined fans at a party in the parking lot. Some children, and even a few grown-ups, painted their faces for the game!

As fans made their way
through the stadium gates, they
cheered, "Let's go, Panthers!"

The team gathered in the locker room before the game. Players strapped on their pads and dressed in their Carolina Panthers uniforms.

The coach delivered final instructions and encouraged the team to play their best. The coach cheered, "Let's go, Panthers!"

It was now time for the Carolina Panthers to take the field. The announcer called, "Ladies and gentlemen, please welcome your Carolina Panthers!" The Panthers sprinted onto the field and were greeted by their loyal fans. It was very loud in the stadium!

The Panthers huddled around the team captains and cheered, "Let's go, Panthers!"

The team captains met at midfield for the coin toss. The referee flipped a coin high in the air and the visiting team called, "Heads." The coin landed with the heads side up – the Panthers would begin the game by kicking off.

The referee reminded the players that it was important to play hard, but also with good sportsmanship.

The Panthers kicker booted the ball down the field to start the action. With the game underway, the kicker cheered, "Let's go, Panthers!"

After the opening kickoff, it was time for the Panthers defense to take the field. Sir Purr led the crowd in a "DE-FENSE" chant. One fan held up a "D" in one hand and a picket fence in the other. With the crowd's encouragement, the Panthers defense sacked the quarterback. Fans appreciated the great play and cheered, "Let's go, Panthers!"

After the defense did its job, the Panthers offense went to work. With great teamwork, they marched down the field. On fourth down, the team was only one yard away from the end zone.

"Let's go for it!" instructed the coach, and the quarterback called a play in the huddle.

The quarterback yelled, "Down. Set. Hike!" before handing the ball to the running back, who crossed the goal line.

TOUCHDOWN!

After the score, the crowd erupted with joy and fans cheered, "Let's go, Panthers!"

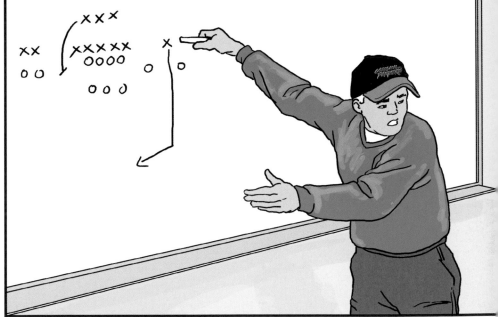

At the end of the first half, the Panthers headed back to the locker room. The coach stopped to answer a few questions from a television reporter. In the locker room, the team rested and prepared for the second half.

Meanwhile, Panthers fans stretched
their legs and picked up a few snacks at the
concession stands. In the concourse, Panthers
fans cheered, "Let's go, Panthers!"

In the second half, the temperature dropped and rain began to fall. The team played hard through the storm. Young Panthers fans drank hot chocolate to help them stay warm. One little fan was surprised to see herself on the big screen. With everybody watching, she cheered, "Let's go, Panthers!"

With only a few seconds remaining, the score was tied. The Panthers lined-up for a field goal try. After a good snap and a perfect hold, the kicker booted the ball toward the goal posts. The stadium was nearly silent as all eyes followed the flight of the ball.

The kick was good!

The Carolina Panthers won the football game! The kicker cheered, "Let's go, Panthers!"

To celebrate the thrilling victory, Panthers players dumped water on the coach. The teams shook hands and congratulated each other on a good game. As Panthers fans left the stadium, they cheered, "Let's go, Panthers!"

For Anna and Maya.~ Aimee Aryal

For Sue, Ana Milagros, and Angel Miguel. ~ Miguel De Angel

www.panthers.com

For more information, please contact Mascot Books,
P.O. Box 220157, Chantilly, VA 20153-0157

CAROLINA PANTHERS, PANTHERS, and SIR PURR
are trademarks or registered trademarks of The Carolina Panthers.

ISBN: 978-1-932888-97-3

Printed in the United States.

www.mascotbooks.com

Title List

Team	Book Title	Author	Team	Book Title	Author
Baseball			**Pro Football**		
Boston Red Sox	Hello, Wally!	Jerry Remy	Carolina Panthers	Let's Go, Panthers!	Aimee Aryal
Boston Red Sox	Wally And His Journey Through Red Sox Nation!	Jerry Remy	Dallas Cowboys	How 'Bout Them Cowboys!	Aimee Aryal
New York Yankees	Let's Go, Yankees!	Yogi Berra	Green Bay Packers	Go, Packres, Go!	Aimee Aryal
New York Mets	Hello, Mr. Met!	Rusty Staub	Kansas City Chiefs	Let's Go, Chiefs!	Aimee Aryal
St. Louis Cardinals	Hello, Fredbird!	Ozzie Smith	Minnesota Vikings	Let's Go, Vikings!	Aimee Aryal
Philadelphia Phillies	Hello, Phillie Phanatic!	Aimee Aryal	New York Giants	Let's Go, Giants!	Aimee Aryal
Chicago Cubs	Let's Go, Cubs!	Aimee Aryal	New England Patriots	Let's Go, Patriots!	Aimee Aryal
Chicago White Sox	Let's Go, White Sox!	Aimee Aryal	Seattle Seahawks	Let's Go, Seahawks!	Aimee Aryal
Cleveland Indians	Hello, Slider!	Bob Feller	Washington Redskins	Hail To The Redskins!	Aimee Aryal
			Coloring Book		
			Dallas Cowboys	How 'Bout Them Cowboys!	Aimee Aryal
College					
Alabama	Hello, Big Al!	Aimee Aryal	Michigan State	Hello, Sparty!	Aimee Aryal
Alabama	Roll Tide!	Ken Stabler	Minnesota	Hello, Goldy!	Aimee Aryal
Arizona	Hello, Wilbur!	Lute Olsen	Mississippi	Hello, Colonel Rebel!	Aimee Aryal
Arkansas	Hello, Big Red!	Aimee Aryal	Mississippi State	Hello, Bully!	Aimee Aryal
Auburn	Hello, Aubie!	Aimee Aryal	Missouri	Hello, Truman!	Todd Donoho
Auburn	War Eagle!	Pat Dye	Nebraska	Hello, Herbie Husker!	Aimee Aryal
Boston College	Hello, Baldwin!	Aimee Aryal	North Carolina	Hello, Rameses!	Aimee Aryal
Brigham Young	Hello, Cosmo!	LaVell Edwards	North Carolina St.	Hello, Mr. Wuf!	Aimee Aryal
Clemson	Hello, Tiger!	Aimee Aryal	Notre Dame	Let's Go, Irish!	Aimee Aryal
Colorado	Hello, Ralphie!	Aimee Aryal	Ohio State	Hello, Brutus!	Aimee Aryal
Connecticut	Hello, Jonathan!	Aimee Aryal	Oklahoma	Let's Go, Sooners!	Aimee Aryal
Duke	Hello, Blue Devil!	Aimee Aryal	Oklahoma State	Hello, Pistol Pete!	Aimee Aryal
Florida	Hello, Albert!	Aimee Aryal	Penn State	Hello, Nittany Lion!	Aimee Aryal
Florida State	Let's Go, 'Noles!	Aimee Aryal	Penn State	We Are Penn State!	Joe Paterno
Georgia	Hello, Hairy Dawg!	Aimee Aryal	Purdue	Hello, Purdue Pete!	Aimee Aryal
Georgia	How 'Bout Them Dawgs!	Vince Dooley	Rutgers	Hello, Scarlet Knight!	Aimee Aryal
Georgia Tech	Hello, Buzz!	Aimee Aryal	South Carolina	Hello, Cocky!	Aimee Aryal
Illinois	Let's Go, Illini!	Aimee Aryal	So. California	Hello, Tommy Trojan!	Aimee Aryal
Indiana	Let's Go, Hoosiers!	Aimee Aryal	Syracuse	Hello, Otto!	Aimee Aryal
Iowa	Hello, Herky!	Aimee Aryal	Tennessee	Hello, Smokey!	Aimee Aryal
Iowa State	Hello, Cy!	Amy DeLashmutt	Texas	Hello, Hook 'Em!	Aimee Aryal
James Madison	Hello, Duke Dog!	Aimee Aryal	Texas A & M	Howdy, Reveille!	Aimee Aryal
Kansas	Hello, Big Jay!	Aimee Aryal	UCLA	Hello, Joe Bruin!	Aimee Aryal
Kansas State	Hello, Willie!	Dan Walter	Virginia	Hello, CavMan!	Aimee Aryal
Kentucky	Hello, Wildcat!	Aimee Aryal	Virginia Tech	Hello, Hokie Bird!	Aimee Aryal
Louisiana State	Hello, Mike!	Aimee Aryal	Virginia Tech	Yea, It's Hokie Game Day!	Frank Beamer
Maryland	Hello, Testudo!	Aimee Aryal	Wake Forest	Hello, Demon Deacon!	Aimee Aryal
Michigan	Let's Go, Blue!	Aimee Aryal	West Virginia	Hello, Mountaineer!	Aimee Aryal
			Wisconsin	Hello, Bucky!	Aimee Aryal

NBA

Dallas Mavericks	Let's Go, Mavs!	Mark Cuban

Kentucky Derby

Kentucky Derby	White Diamond Runs For The Roses	Aimee Aryal

More great titles coming soon!

info@mascotbooks.com